For Tess and her hamster Zintan

- An

First published in Belgium and Holland by Clavis Uitgeverij, Hasselt – Amsterdam, 2016
Copyright © 2016, Clavis Uitgeverij

English translation from the Dutch by Clavis Publishing Inc. New York
Copyright © 2017 for the English language edition: Clavis Publishing Inc. New York

Visit us on the web at www.clavisbooks.com

Santa, Please Bring Me a Gnome written by An Swerts and illustrated by Eline van Lindenhuizen
Original title: *Krijg ik een kabouter, Sint?*
Translated from the Dutch by Clavis Publishing

ISBN 978-1-60537-275-4 (hardback edition)
ISBN 978-1-60537-389-8 (paperback edition)

This book was printed in June 2017 at Publikum d.o.o., Slavka Rodica 6, Belgrade, Serbia

First Edition
10 9 8 7 6 5 4 3 2 1

Clavis Publishing supports the First Amendment and celebrates the right to read

Santa, Please Bring Me a Gnome

An Swerts & Eline van Lindenhuizen

"Tess, feel how soft he is!"
Mom says, taking a giant teddy bear in her arms.
"And look over there, that little doctor's bag!
Or that toadstool, what a cute lamp!"

Tess shrugs. She already knows what
she's going to ask Santa to bring her.

"Granny, will you write my letter to Santa?"
"Of course!" Grandma says.
"Dear Santa," Tess starts. "You don't have to bring me any toys this year."
Grandma lays down her pen. "Did I just hear that right?" she asks.
But Tess continues: "The only thing I want is *a real gnome*."
"Gosh," says Grandma. "That's *the best wish ever!*"

"Grandpa, I need a lot of things!" Tess calls out as she runs into Grandpa's shed.
"A small bed, a small table, a little chair and wardrobe…."
"Wow!" Grandpa laughs. "Are you going to redecorate your room?"
Tess beams. "No, Grandpa, it's **not for me**; it's for a gnome!"
"A gnome!" Grandpa repeats. "Then we need to get cracking!"

Grandpa makes the *sweetest little pieces of furniture*,
and Grandma sews a teeny *tiny patchwork* quilt.
She gives Tess a ball of cotton too.
"Then he has something soft to sleep on," she smiles.

And as Tess puts the furniture in the dollhouse,
she thinks about how fun it will be to have a friend with her always.

A friend to go to **school** with her…

… and to **dance class**.

A friend to sit on the **swings** with…

… to do **crafts** with…

… to *eat* with…

… and to *read* with.

A friend she can even take with her in the *bathtub*…

… and into dreamland,
in his own *little bed*.

Santa is coming tonight… **_and so is the gnome_**!
He'll probably be hungry after such a long trip.
So Tess puts out a slice of orange for him.

"We're very curious to see what Santa is going to bring you," says Dad.
"Don't you want *to tell us* what it is yet?"
"No, but I'm sure you'll love it as much as I do!" Tess laughs.

The following morning, Tess wakes up with *butterflies in her belly*.
Santa! Santa was here last night!

Full of anticipation, Tess comes down the stairs.
Ohhh… *the dollhouse is empty*;
             all the furniture is gone!

Tess feels tears pricking her eyes
but Mom points to the corner of the room….

There's a big glass box in the corner, filled with sawdust.
And next to the box there's… a letter! "Shall I read it to you?" Mom asks.
Tess can only nod.

Dear Tess, you are a very sweet girl and I really wanted to bring you a gnome.
But it just didn't work out; let me tell you why.
Gerard the Gnome was looking forward to coming and living with you.
His little suitcase was packed and ready to go.
But then someone knocked on his door, and there stood…

... *Flannel*, with trembling whiskers and moist eyes.
His home was destroyed and his winter stores stolen.
He sprained his little paw, had a bad cold and....
In short, all the bad luck that can happen to a hamster happened to him.

So Flannel really needed a nice, warm place to stay,
with someone who would take good care of him.
And that's why Gerard the Gnome thought of you.

Tess looks curiously into the box. Oh my, the little quilt is moving!
And oh, look at the sweet little face that appears! "Hi, Flannel,"
Tess says softly, at which the hamster looks at her with shiny little eyes.
Tess gets a warm feeling inside.
How kind of Gerard the Gnome and Santa!

Tess and Flannel become *the best of friends*.
When Tess puts her hands in the box,
the hamster crawls into the palm of her hand.

And as she tells Flannel what happened at school and in dance class,
she softly pets him. He loves that. And he listens like *a real friend*.